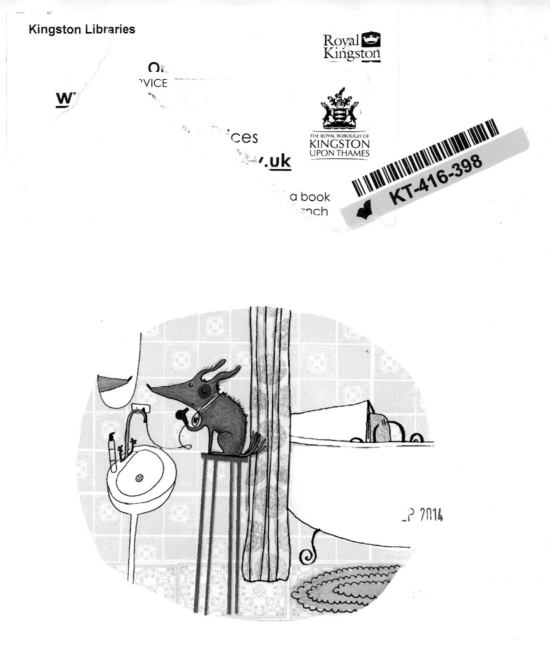

_P 2014

For my Pierre-like adventure
companions Mez and Yesim

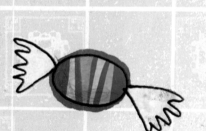

Bloomsbury Publishing, London, New Delhi, New York and Sydney

First published in Great Britain in 2014 by Bloomsbury Publishing Plc
50 Bedford Square, London, WC1B 3DP

Text and Illustrations copyright © Catalina Echeverri 2014
The moral right of the author/illustrator has been asserted

A CIP catalogue record for this book is available from the British Library

ISBN 978 1 4088 3938 6 (HB)
ISBN 978 1 4088 3939 3 (PB)
ISBN 978 1 4088 3937 9 (eBook)

Printed in China by C & C Offset Printing Co Ltd, Shenzhen, Guangdong

1 3 5 7 9 10 8 6 4 2

www.bloomsbury.com

It's not easy being inconspicuous (that means being almost invisible)
when you are a big green French dinosaur with a curly black moustache.

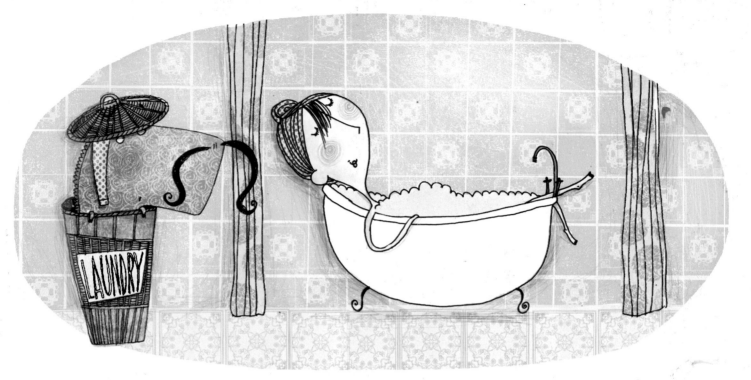

But, thankfully, Pierre is **very** good at hiding.

In fact, Pierre is SO good at hiding,

that no one can see him.

Nobody, that is, except . . .

ME!

SUPER DUPER EXTRA cheesy POPCORN

I love having Pierre around.
With Pierre, life is never boring . . .

Every Tuesday we travel to the moon
and drink hot galactic chocolate
with marshmallow stars.

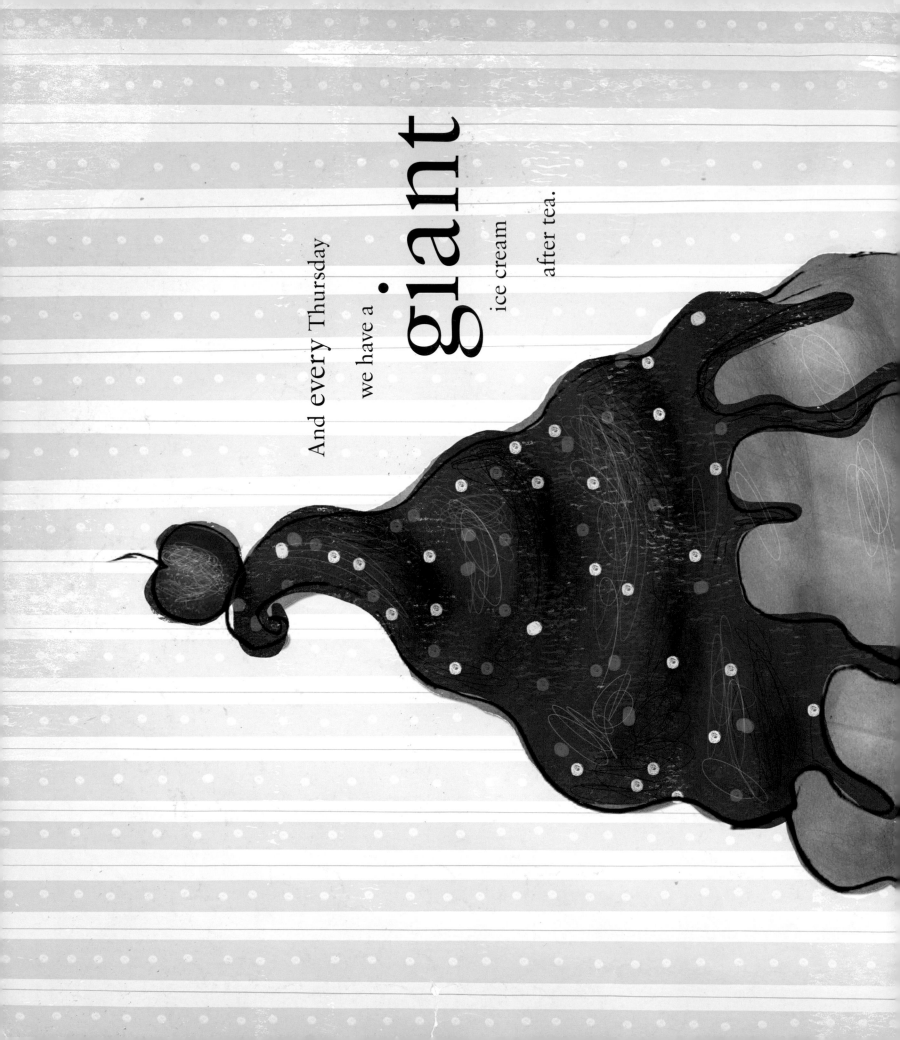

And every Thursday we have a **giant** ice cream after tea.

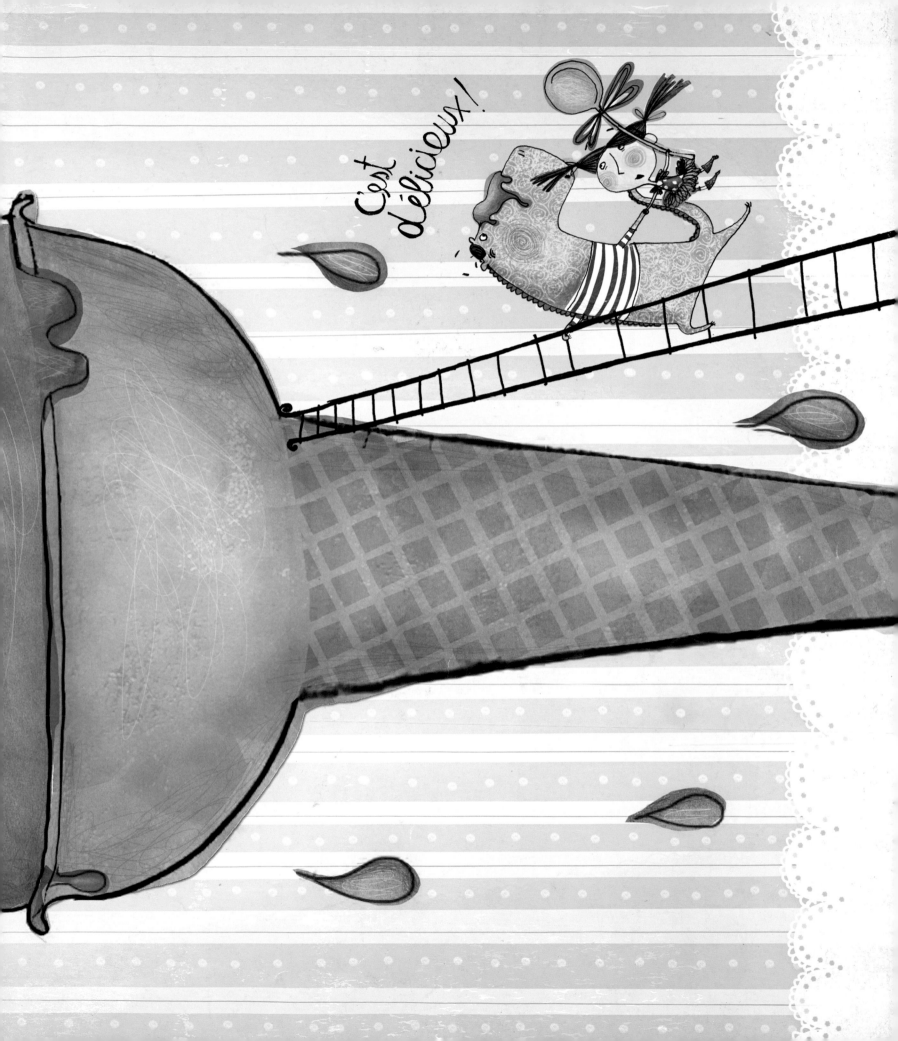

La-la

When it rains, we don't mind.
We stay indoors and dance upside down
to the tune of Pierre's magic violin.

la-lee-lee!

And when it's sunny,

we sail in our bathtub boat
to magical lands . . .

Lands where the trees are made from candyfloss and where you can be taken on a sweetie tasting tour by a jelly bear in a cowboy hat.

I have SO much
fun with Pierre.

wheeeeee

I'd like him to stay
forever . . .

But everyone knows that French dinosaurs like Pierre only get to stay in people's bathtubs for the summer.

So, when the leaves start to fall off the trees, it's time for Pierre to pack up his suitcase.

Before he goes, we have a delicious picnic
with plenty of stinky cheese –
Pierre's favourite!

100% STINK FREE CHEESE

Then we say goodbye,
promising to write often.
Pierre says that he will be back
VERY soon . . .

à bientôt

and I believe him!

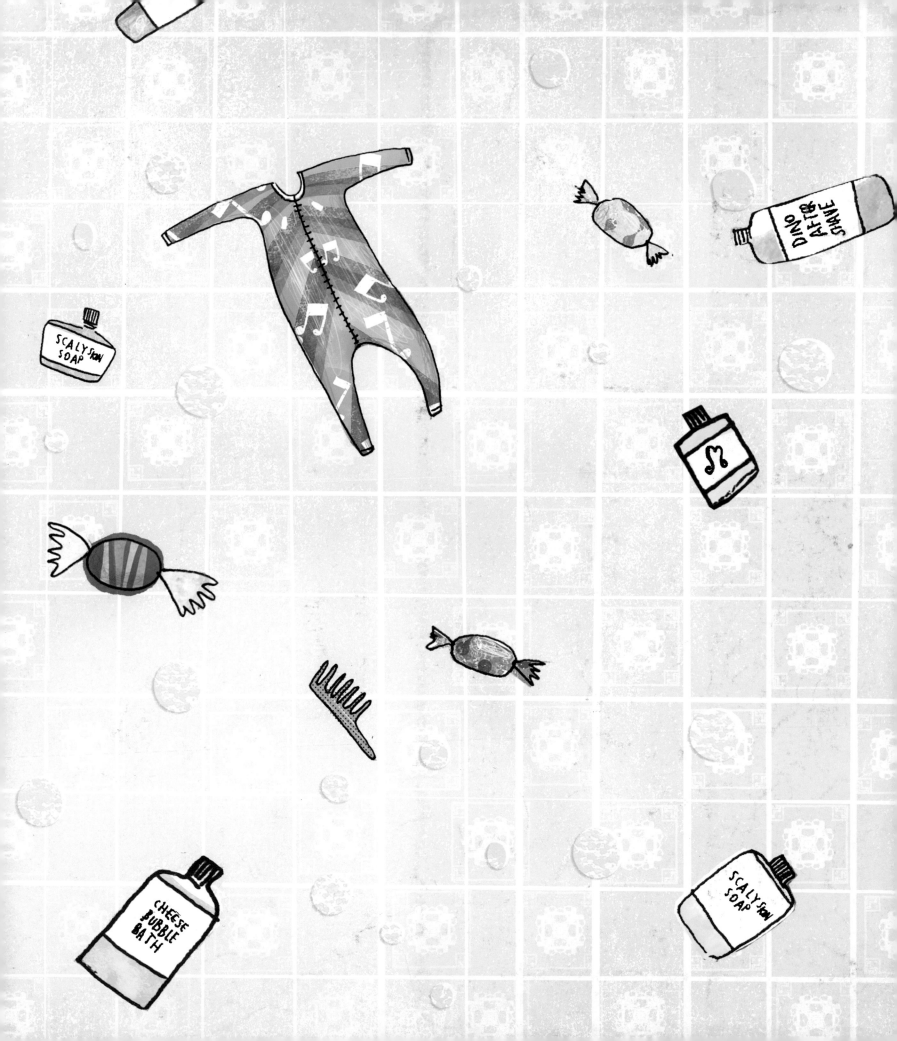